Cambridge Early Years

Communication and Language

for English as a Second Language

Learner's Book 3B

Claire Medwell

Contents

Note to parents and practitioners   3

Block 3: Caring for ourselves and the world   4

Block 4: Then and now   18

Acknowledgements   32

Note to parents and practitioners

This Learner's Book provides activities to support the second term of ESL Communication and Language for Cambridge Early Years 3.

Activities can be used at school or at home. Children will need support from an adult. Additional guidance about activities can be found in the **For practitioners** boxes.

Stories are provided for children to enjoy looking at and listening to. Children are not expected to be able to read the stories themselves.

Children will encounter the following characters within this book. You could ask children to point to the characters when they see them on the pages, and say their names.

The Learner's Book activities support the Teaching Resource activities. The Teaching Resource provides step-by-step coverage of the Cambridge Early Years curriculum and guidance on how the Learner's Book activities develop the curriculum learning statements.

Hi, my name is Mia.

Find us on the front covers doing lots of fun activities.

Hi, my name is Gemi.

Hi, my name is Rafi.

Hi, my name is Kiho.

Block 3
Caring for ourselves and the world

Sadi's Sunset by Alex Eeles

Sadi is a **small** hyena with a **BIG** plan.

Today, she is going to leave her home by the tall tree and walk OVER the dusty plains, ACROSS the deep river, THROUGH the thick forest, UP the steep hill, ALL THE WAY to the round rock!

She wants to see the sunset. And everyone says the rock is the best place to go.

As she leaves, Sadi meets her friend Ayla. "Where are you going?" asks Ayla.

"To the round rock to see the sunset," replies Sadi. "Do you want to come?"

"Yes please!"

But when they reach the dusty plains, Ayla stops.

"Monkeys do not like walking," she says. "We like swinging through the trees."

Soon, Sadi meets her friend Dilan.
"Where are you going?" he asks.
"To the round rock to see the sunset," replies Sadi.
"Do you want to come?"
"Yes please!"

But when they reach the deep river, Dilan stops.
"Giraffes do not like swimming," he says.
"We like walking on dry land."

Soon, Sadi meets her friend Lora.
"Where are you going?" she asks.
"To the round rock to see the sunset," replies Sadi.
"Do you want to come?"
"Yes please!"
But when they reach the thick forest, Lora stops.

"Hippos do not like squeezing between trees," she says.
"We like relaxing in the water."

Soon, Sadi meets her friend Nate.
"Where are you going?" he asks.
"To the round rock to see the sunset," replies Sadi.
"Do you want to come?"
"Yes please!"

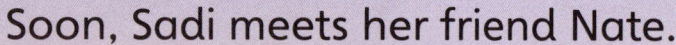

But when they reach the steep hill, Nate stops.
"Honey badgers don't like being up high," he says. "We like hiding underground."
UP, UP, UP Sadi climbs!
Until at last she reaches the round rock.
Just in time for sunset.
It is BEAUTIFUL!

If only my friends could see it too, thinks Sadi.
Which gives her an idea.
Off she runs … DOWN the steep hill, THROUGH the thick forest, ACROSS the deep river and OVER the dusty plains.
ALL THE WAY to her house by the tall tree!
That night, Sadi stays up working on a new plan.

And the next day, she takes a gift to each of her friends … so they can all see the sunset any time they want!

What am I?

Look and colour.

Find the animals from the story. Colour them in.

hyena

frog

fox

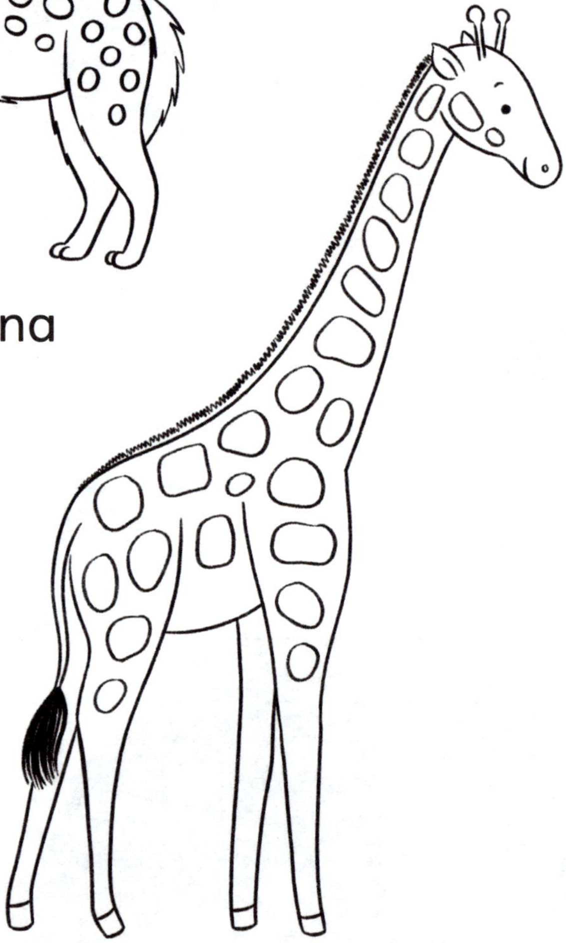

giraffe

monkey

For practitioners

Invite children to look closely at each of the animal pictures and encourage them to identify each one. Ask *Which animals are not in the story?* Point to and read each label with the children. They then colour in the three animals from the story *Sadi's Sunset*, referring to the story pages for help.

Animal activities

Say and match.

Match each animal to what it likes to do.

For practitioners
Children say the name of each animal and then match them to the things they like doing. Encourage children to talk about the activities that the animals like or don't like doing, e.g., *The monkey likes swinging through the trees.*

A nature scene

Look and draw.

Draw each feature from the box to complete the picture.

a hill   trees   a big rock   a river   a field

For practitioners
Invite children to observe the landscape picture. Then ask them to add some elements to the picture, using the smaller pictures in the box as a reference. Children may like to describe their scene using *here* and *there*. They may also like to label their scenes with simple, factual information.

Five Little Green Frogs (Traditional rhyme)

Five little green frogs,
Sat on a speckled log.
Eating the most delicious grub … YUM YUM!
One jumped into the pool,
Where it was nice and cool!
Now there are four little green frogs.

Four little green frogs …
Three little green frogs …
Two little green frogs …
One little green frog …

… Now there are no more little green frogs!

A frog's life

Point and say.
What is happening in each picture?

For practitioners
Invite children to talk about what is happening in each picture. Check for understanding by asking *Is the frog sleeping? Is the frog eating an insect? What is this frog doing?*

Five little frogs

Draw and say.

Add three more frogs to the log.

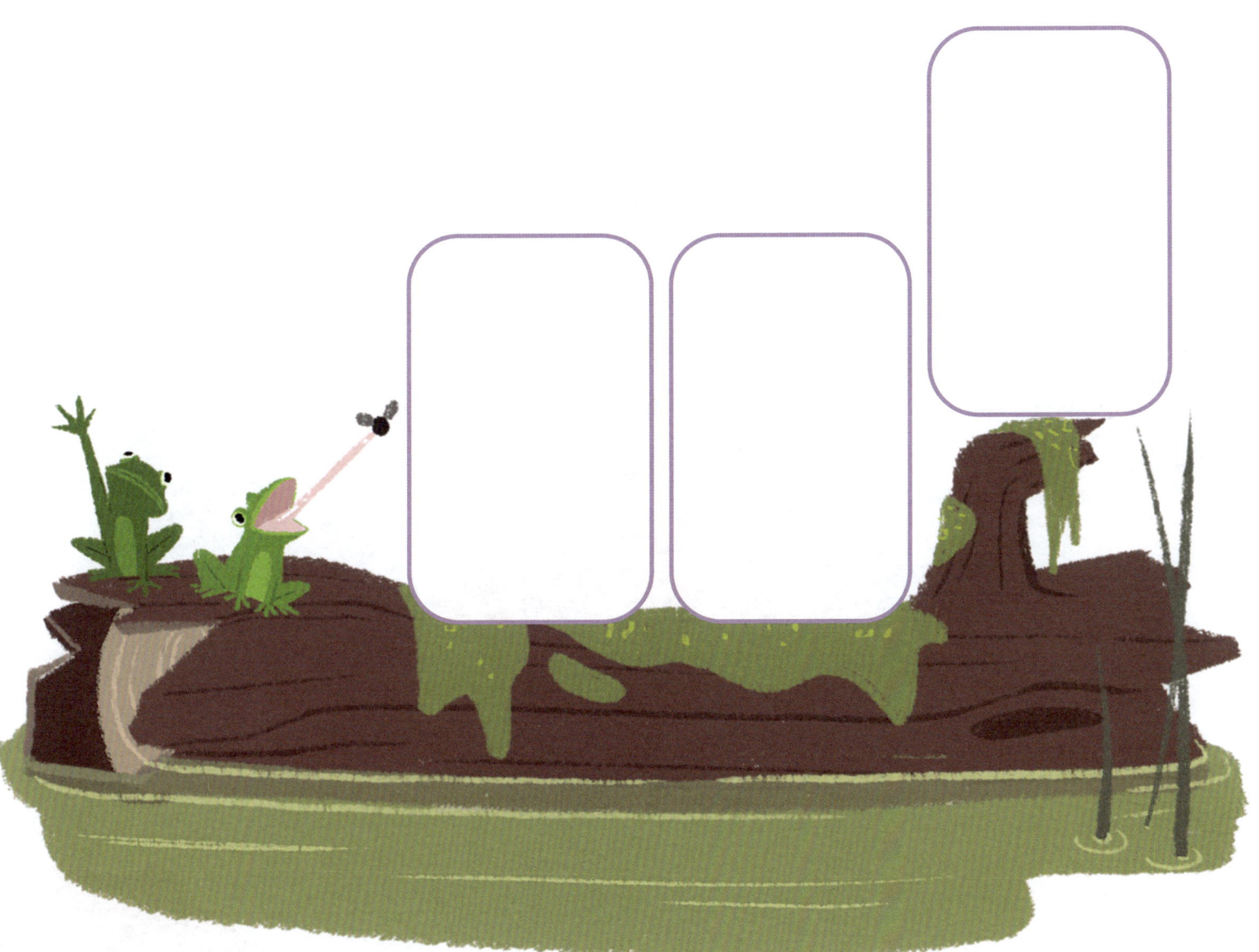

For practitioners

Ask children to say what the two frogs are doing. Then encourage them to think of other actions that a frog could be doing, e.g., playing, jumping, etc. They then draw three more frogs doing different actions. Ask children to talk about what they have drawn and prompt them with the necessary language and simple everyday phrases.

Block 4 Then and now

Rex's Sore Throat by Alex Eeles

When Rex woke up, the first thing he said was …

OUCH!

Actually, he didn't *say* **OUCH**, he *whispered* it.
In his quietest, croakiest voice.
Rex had a VERY sore throat.

So sore that he couldn't eat any breakfast.
So sore that he couldn't go to school.
So sore that he stayed in bed all day!

In the afternoon, Rex's friend Hazel came to see him.
"Perhaps you have a cold," she said.
Hazel gave Rex a hot water bottle and made him a mug of honey and lemon tea.

Being looked after was nice.
But the next morning, Rex's throat hurt even more.
He stayed in bed all day again.

After school, Rex's friend Lance came to see him.
"Maybe you have a fever," he said.
He felt Rex's forehead and took his temperature.
It was normal.
Rex was glad not to have a fever.

But the next morning, his throat was more sore than ever.
He couldn't even manage a whisper.
He stayed in bed all day. AGAIN!
That night, the doctor came to see him.

"Do you have a cough?" she asked.
Rex shook his head.
"A stomach ache?"
Rex shook his head.
"A headache?"
Rex shook his head.
"Hmmmm," said the doctor.

She leaned in to listen to Rex's chest.

Her long hair tickled his nose.
Rex tried to hold it in, but it was no good.
AH … AH … AH …

ACHOOO!

He sneezed loudly.

And as he did so, an enormous jet of flames flew out of his mouth and nose!

After a few minutes, the flames went out.

Rex realised the pain in his throat had gone too!

"It seems like all that fire was the problem!" smiled the doctor.
"Just make sure you breathe it out every day from now on."
"I will!" replied Rex.
He couldn't wait to tell his friends what had happened.

"I do have one bit of bad news though," said the doctor.
"You're going to need some new curtains!"

What's the matter?

Join the dots.

Complete the picture.
Say what is wrong with each animal.

For practitioners
Encourage children to point to and name the different illnesses the animals have in the picture. Ask *What's the matter with (Rex)? Who can help (Rex) feel better?* Invite children to join the dots then colour in to complete the picture and reveal who will help all the animals (*the doctor*).

A visit to the doctor

Look and say.

Look at the pictures. Say what is happening.

For practitioners

Encourage children to identify where the girl is and what common illness she has. Draw their attention to the words in the speech bubbles and ask them to repeat the conversation with you. They may like to act out the scene using the actual words or their own ideas.

Get well soon!

Listen and number.

Listen to the story.
Number the pictures in the right order.

For practitioners
Look at the pictures and explain they are in the wrong order. Read the story again and ask children to listen carefully. As they listen, they number the pictures in the correct order. Encourage children to use the joined pictures to retell the story.

Doctor, doctor!
Please come quick!
Little Baby is sick, sick, sick!

Her tummy hurts, boo, hoo, hoo!
Doctor doctor,
please come quick!

Doctor arrives and
the doctor says
"Rest little baby,
Get well soon!"

Baby is sick

Think and match.

Match each label to the part of Baby that hurts.

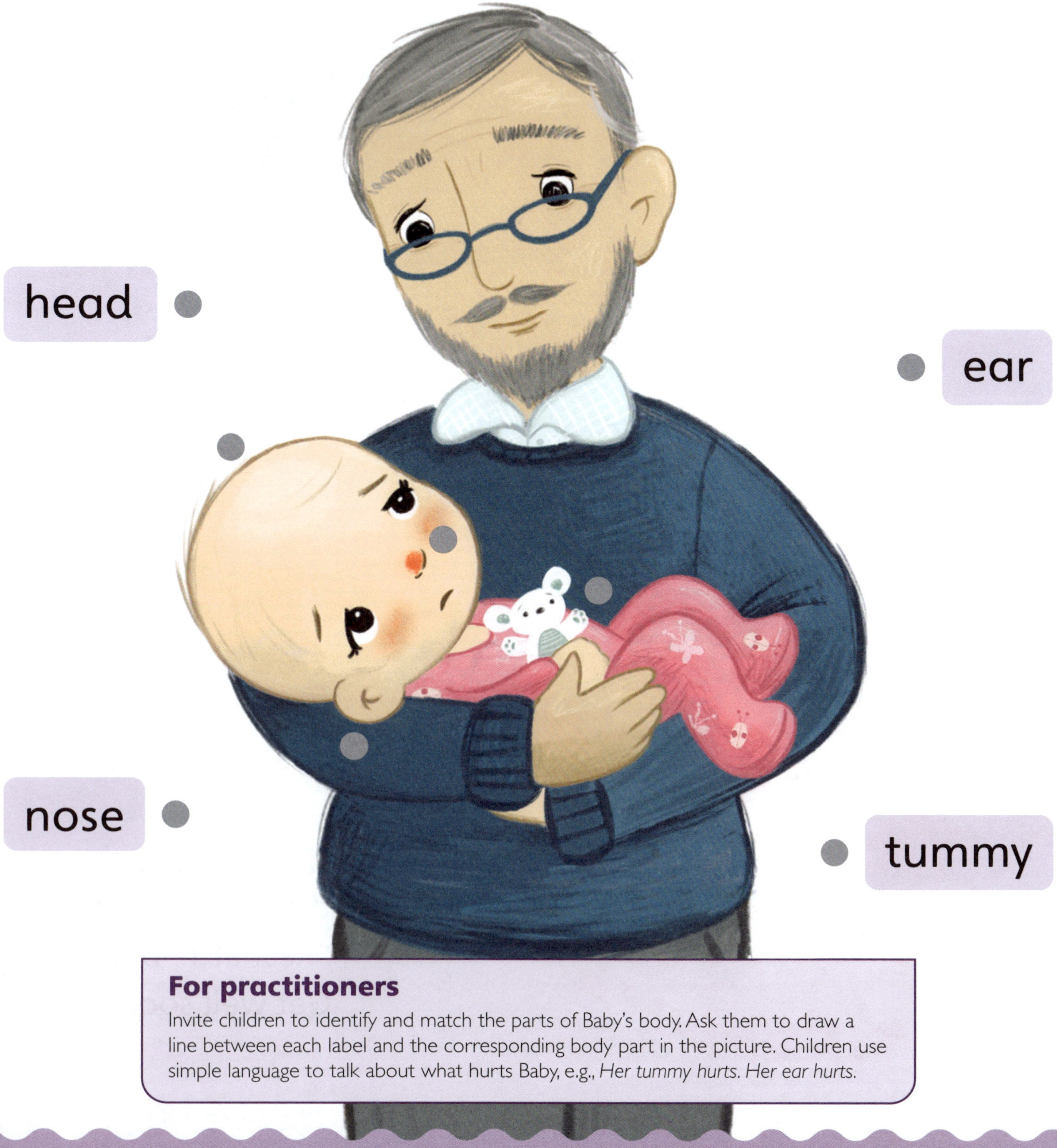

head •

• ear

nose •

• tummy

For practitioners

Invite children to identify and match the parts of Baby's body. Ask them to draw a line between each label and the corresponding body part in the picture. Children use simple language to talk about what hurts Baby, e.g., *Her tummy hurts. Her ear hurts.*

Picture order

Match and say.

Match the pictures to the correct speech bubbles.

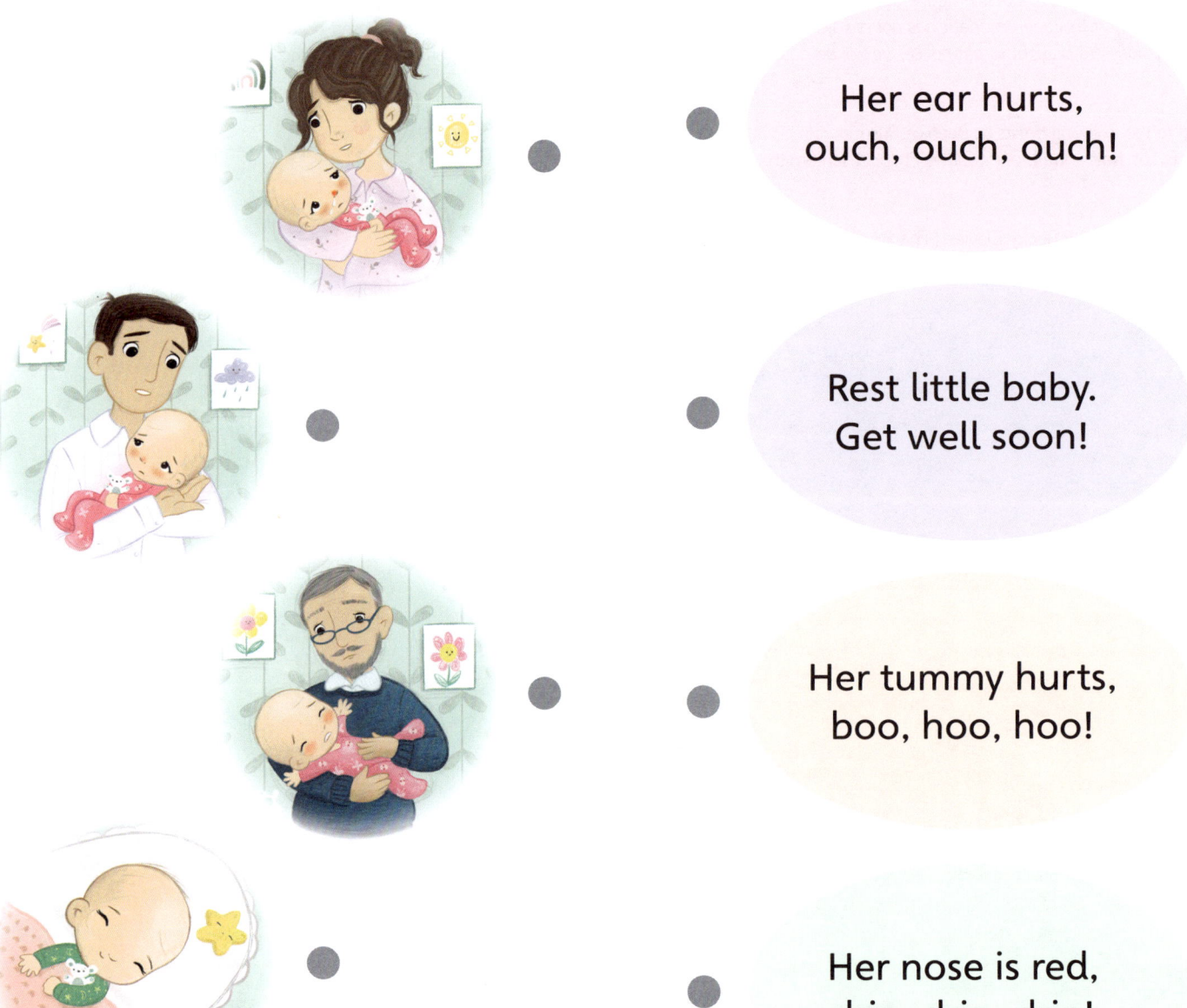

For practitioners

Play or sing the *Baby is Sick* song and encourage children to join in. Ask them to look carefully at the pictures and to draw lines to match each picture with the correct speech bubble.

Acknowledgements

The authors and publishers acknowledge the following sources of copyright material and are grateful for the permissions granted.
While every effort has been made, it has not always been possible to identify the sources of all the material used, or to trace all copyright holders.
If any omissions are brought to our notice, we will be happy to include the appropriate acknowledgements on reprinting.

Thanks to the following artists at Beehive Illustration:
Chloe Evans, Katharine Henry, Claire Philpott, Jan Smith.

Cover characters by Becky Davies (The Bright Agency)

Let's get active!
Spot the difference.
Look at the pictures. Find four differences.

> **For practitioners**
> Encourage children to work with a partner and talk about what is happening in the pictures. Tell them there are four differences and invite them to find and describe them.

Baby is Sick

(song to the tune of *Five Little Monkeys Jumping on the Bed*)

Doctor, doctor!
Please come quick!
Little Baby is sick, sick, sick!

Her nose is red, drip, drip, drip!
Doctor doctor,
please come quick!

Doctor arrives and the doctor says
"Rest little baby,
Get well soon!"

Doctor, doctor!
Please come quick!
Little Baby is sick, sick, sick!

Her ear hurts, ouch, ouch, ouch!
Doctor doctor,
please come quick!

Doctor arrives and the doctor says
"Rest little baby,
Get well soon!"